For someone speshal,
with hums from
a dear friend

POSITIVELY POOH

Timeless Wisdom from Pooh

DUTTON CHILDREN'S BOOKS
A division of Penguin Young Readers Group

Published by the Penguin Group
Penguin Group (USA) Inc., 375 Hudson Street, New York, New York 10014, U.S.A.
Penguin Group (Canada), 90 Eglinton Avenue East, Suite 700, Toronto, Ontario, Canada M4P 2Y3 (a division of Pearson Penguin
Canada Inc.) • Penguin Books Ltd, 80 Strand, London WC2R 0RL, England • Penguin Ireland, 25 St Stephen's Green, Dublin 2,
Ireland (a division of Penguin Books Ltd) • Penguin Group (Australia), 250 Camberwell Road, Camberwell, Victoria 3124, Australia
(a division of Pearson Australia Group Pty Ltd) • Penguin Books India Pvt Ltd, 11 Community Centre, Panchsheel Park, New Delhi -
110 017, India • Penguin Group (NZ), 67 Apollo Drive, Rosedale, North Shore 0745, Auckland, New Zealand (a division of Pearson
New Zealand Ltd) • Penguin Books (South Africa) (Pty) Ltd, 24 Sturdee Avenue, Rosebank, Johannesburg 2196, South Africa
Penguin Books Ltd, Registered Offices: 80 Strand, London WC2R 0RL, England

This book is a work of fiction. Names, characters, places, and incidents are either the product of the author's imagination or are used
fictitiously, and any resemblance to actual persons, living or dead, business establishments, events, or locales is entirely coincidental.

Selected text from *Winnie-the-Pooh* and *The House At Pooh Corner* by A. A. Milne copyright © 2007 by Michael John Brown,
Peter Janson-Smith, Roger Hugh Vaughan Charles Morgan, and Timothy Michael Robinson, Trustees of the Pooh Properties

Line illustrations copyright © E. H. Shepard
Coloring of the illustrations copyright © 1970, 1973, and 1974 by E. H. Shepard and Egmont UK Limited

The Pooh Sketchbook copyright © 1982 Lloyds TSB Bank Ltd., Executors of the Estate of E. H. Shepard, and the E. H. Shepard Trust

Book design and new text copyright © Egmont UK Limited

The publisher does not have any control over and does not assume any responsibility for author or third-party websites or their content.

CIP DATA IS AVAILABLE.

Published in the United States 2008 by Dutton Children's Books,
a division of Penguin Young Readers Group
345 Hudson Street, New York, New York 10014
www.penguin.com/youngreaders

Originally published in Great Britain 2007 by Egmont Books Limited, London

Printed in Singapore • First American Edition
ISBN 978-0-525-47931-4
1 3 5 7 9 10 8 6 4 2

POSITIVELY POOH

Timeless Wisdom from Pooh

A. A. MILNE ◆ *Decorations by* ERNEST H. SHEPARD

Dutton Children's Books

Contents

CHAPTER ONE

For your inner bear

Allow enough time for a morning wash!

Roo was washing his face and paws in the stream, while Kanga explained to everybody proudly that this was the first time he had ever washed his face himself, and Owl was telling Kanga an Interesting Anecdote full of long words like Encyclopaedia and Rhododendron to which Kanga wasn't listening.

"I don't hold with all this washing," grumbled Eeyore. "This modern Behind-the-ears nonsense. What do *you* think, Pooh?"

When did you **last** have
a thorough **check-up?**

why! what's happened to your
tail?

"Let's have a look at you," said Pooh.

So Eeyore stood there, gazing sadly at the ground, and Winnie-the-Pooh walked all round him once.

"Why, what's happened to your tail?" he said in surprise.

"What *has* happened to it?" said Eeyore.

"It isn't there!"

"Are you sure?"

"Well, either a tail *is* there or it isn't there. You can't make a mistake about it. And yours *isn't* there!"

"Then what is?"

"Nothing."

Find a type of exercise
to suit you.

Balancing on three legs, he began to bring his
fourth leg very cautiously up to his ear.

"I did this yesterday," he explained, as he
fell down for the third time. "It's quite easy. . . ."

Don't try too hard;
let the hums get *you*.

"Poetry and Hums aren't things
which you get, they're things which
get you. And all you can do is to go
where they can find you."

Winnie the Pooh

"He climbed and he climbed"

Stop to **pass** the
time of day.

"I make it seventeen days come Friday since anybody spoke to me."

"It certainly isn't seventeen days—"

"Come Friday," explained Eeyore.

"And today's Saturday," said Rabbit. "So that would make it eleven days. And I was here myself a week ago."

"Not conversing," said Eeyore. "Not first one and then the other. You said 'Hallo' and Flashed Past. I saw your tail in the distance as I was meditating my reply. I had thought of saying 'What?' —but, of course, it was then too late."

"Well, I was in a hurry."

Think about all the **exciting**
things that are going
to happen today
(particularly on
Monday mornings).

"When you wake up in the morning, Pooh,"
said Piglet at last, "what's the first thing
you say to yourself?"

"What's for breakfast?" said Pooh. "What
do *you* say, Piglet?"

"I say, I wonder what's going to happen
exciting *today*?" said Piglet.

Pooh nodded thoughtfully.

"It's the same thing," he said.

Always have a plan Bee.

"What do I look like?"

"You look like a Bear holding on to a balloon," you said.

"Not—" said Pooh anxiously, "—not like a small black cloud in a blue sky?"

"Not very much."

"Ah, well, perhaps from up here it looks different. And, as I say, you never can tell with bees."

Reduce headaches...

Here is Edward Bear, coming downstairs now, bump, bump, bump, on the back of his head, behind Christopher Robin. It is, as far as he knows, the only way of coming downstairs, but sometimes he feels that there really is another way, if only he could stop bumping for a moment and think of it. And then he feels that perhaps there isn't.

find another way.

Be positive about
meeting new people.

"Hallo, Eeyore!" said Pooh. "This is Tigger."

"What is?" said Eeyore.

"This," explained Pooh and Piglet together, and Tigger smiled his happiest smile and said nothing. Eeyore walked all round Tigger one way, and then turned and walked all round him the other way.

"What did you say it was?" he asked.

"Tigger."

"Ah!" said Eeyore.

"He's just come," explained Piglet.

"Ah!" said Eeyore again.

He thought for a long time and then said: "When is he going?"

Try singing
to warm your soul.

They were out of the snow now, but it was very cold, and to keep themselves warm they sang Pooh's song right through six times, Piglet doing the tiddely-poms and Pooh doing the rest of it, and both of them thumping on the top of the gate with pieces of stick at the proper places. And in a little while they felt much warmer, and were able to talk again.

Everything in moderation.

"As he went home with Pooh"
(Tigger is embarrassed)

Pooh always liked a little something at eleven
o'clock in the morning, and he was very glad
to see Rabbit getting out the plates and mugs; and
when Rabbit said, "Honey or condensed milk with your
bread?" he was so excited that he said, "Both," and
then, so as not to seem greedy, he added,

"But don't bother about the bread, please."

"It all comes, I suppose," he decided, as he said good-bye to the last branch, spun round three times, and flew gracefully into a gorse-bush, "it all comes of *liking* honey so much. Oh, help!"

He crawled out of the gorse-bush, brushed the prickles from his nose, and began to think again.

You can have **too much**
of a **good** thing.

He found a small Tin of
Condensed milk

Modesty is the best policy.

But Pooh's mind had gone back to the day
when he had saved Piglet from the flood,
and everybody had admired him so much; and
as that didn't often happen, he thought he
would like it to happen again. And suddenly,
just as it had come before, an idea came to him.

"Owl," said Pooh. "I have thought of something."

"Astute and Helpful Bear," said Owl.
Pooh looked proud at being called a stout
and helpful bear, and said modestly that
he just happened to think of it.

Learn **new things**
and be inspired.

Suddenly Christopher Robin began to tell Pooh
about some of the things: People called Kings
and Queens and something called Factors, and
a place called Europe, and an island in the middle
of the sea where no ships came, and how you make
a Suction Pump (if you want to), and when Knights
were Knighted, and what comes from Brazil. And Pooh,
his back against one of the sixty-something trees,
and his paws folded in front of him, said "Oh!" and
"I didn't know," and thought how wonderful it would
be to have a Real Brain which could tell you things.
And by-and-by Christopher Robin came to an end
of the things, and was silent, and he sat there looking
out over the world, and wishing it wouldn't stop.

Savor every moment.

"What do you like doing best in the world, Pooh?"
"Well," said Pooh, "what I like best—" and then
he had to stop and think. Because although Eating
Honey was a very good thing to do, there was
a moment just before you began to eat it which
was better than when you were, but he didn't know
what it was called.

"Tiggers don't like honey"

CHAPTER TWO

For those bothersome days

Flowers **brighten up** even the most **bothersome** of days.

Piglet had got up early that morning to pick himself a bunch of violets; and when he had picked them and put them in a pot in the middle of his house, it suddenly came over him that nobody had ever picked Eeyore a bunch of violets, and the more he thought of this, the more he thought how sad it was to be an Animal who had never had a bunch of violets picked for him. So he hurried out again, saying to himself, "Eeyore, Violets," and then "Violets, Eeyore," in case he forgot, because it was that sort of day . . .

Avoid people who will make you miserable.

"It's bad enough," said Eeyore, almost breaking down,
"being miserable myself, what with no presents and no
cake and no candles, and no proper notice taken of me
at all, but if everybody else is going to be miserable too—"

Look **the part** so you'll feel
Ready for **Anything.**

As soon as he saw the Big Boots, Pooh knew
that an Adventure was going to happen, and he
brushed the honey off his nose with the back
of his paw, and spruced himself up as well as
he could, so as to look Ready for Anything.

Those with Brain
don't always know it all.

Owl looked at the notice again. To one of his education the reading of it was easy. "Gon out, Backson. Bisy, Backson"—just the sort of thing you'd expect to see on a notice.

"It is quite clear what has happened, my dear Rabbit," he said. "Christopher Robin has gone out somewhere with Backson. He and Backson are busy together. Have you seen a Backson anywhere about in the Forest lately?"

'Go away

Things are **often better**

than they seem.

BANG!!!???***!!!

Piglet lay there, wondering what had happened. At first he thought that the whole world had blown up; and then he thought that perhaps only the Forest part of it had; and then he thought that perhaps only *he* had, and he was now alone in the moon or somewhere, and would never see Christopher Robin or Pooh or Eeyore again. And then he thought, "Well, even if I'm in the moon, I needn't be face downwards all the time," so he got cautiously up and looked about him. He was still in the Forest!

"Well, that's funny," he thought. "I wonder what that bang was. I couldn't have made such a noise just falling down. And where's my balloon? And what's that small piece of damp rag doing?"

"Bang!"

"Did I really do all that?" Piglet said at last.

"Well," said Pooh, "in poetry—in a piece of poetry—well, you *did* it, Piglet, because the poetry says you did. And that's how people know."

"Oh!" said Piglet. "Because I—I thought I did blinch a little. Just at first. And it says, 'Did he blinch no no.' That's why."

"You only blinched inside," said Pooh, "and that's the bravest way for a Very Small Animal not to blinch that there is."

Piglet sighed with happiness, and began to think about himself. He was BRAVE. . . .

and he squoze

Sometimes you are **wonderful** even when you **don't know** it.

No one is perfect.

. . . Owl, wise though he was in many ways, able to read and write and spell his own name WOL . . . somehow went all to pieces over delicate words like MEASLES and BUTTERED TOAST.

a If isn't a dust
cloth

its my shawl .

wol.

Eeyore, the old grey Donkey, stood by the side of the stream, and looked at himself in the water. "Pathetic," he said. "That's what it is. Pathetic. . . . But nobody minds. Nobody cares. Pathetic, that's what it is."

There was a crackling noise in the bracken behind him, and out came Pooh. . . .

"You seem so sad, Eeyore."

"Sad? Why should I be sad? It's my birthday. The happiest day of the year."

"Your birthday?" said Pooh in great surprise. . . .

"Stay there!" he called to Eeyore, as he turned and hurried back home as quick as he could; for he felt that he must get poor Eeyore a present of some sort at once, and he could always think of a proper one afterwards.

A bad day can
always improve.

"Where was I going? Ah, yes, Eeyore." He got up slowly. And then, suddenly, he remembered. He had eaten Eeyore's birthday present!

"*Bother!*" said Pooh. "What *shall* I do? I *must* give him something."

For a little while he couldn't think of anything. Then he thought: "Well, it's a very nice pot, even if there's no honey in it, and if I washed it clean, and got somebody to write '*A Happy Birthday*' on it, Eeyore could keep things in it, which might be Useful."

You can always remedy
an awful mistake.

Do you remember the last time
you enjoyed yourself?

"Sad? Why should I be sad?"

"That's right," said Eeyore. "Sing. Umty-tiddly, umty-too. Here we go gathering Nuts and May. Enjoy yourself."

"I am," said Pooh.

"Some can," said Eeyore.

Bees and trees will
calm and **soothe.**

One day Rabbit and Piglet were sitting
outside Pooh's front door listening to Rabbit,
and Pooh was sitting with them. It was a
drowsy summer afternoon, and the Forest was
full of gentle sounds, which all seemed to be
saying to Pooh, "Don't listen to Rabbit, listen
to me." So he got into a comfortable position
for not listening to Rabbit, and from time to
time he opened his eyes to say "Ah!" and then
closed them again . . .

Maintain some
youthful enthusiasm.

By the time it came to the edge of the Forest, the
stream had grown up, so that it was almost a river, and,
being grown-up, it did not run and jump and sparkle
along as it used to do when it was younger, but moved
more slowly. For it knew now where it was going, and
it said to itself, "There is no hurry. We shall get there
some day." But all the little streams higher up in the
Forest went this way and that, quickly, eagerly, having
so much to find out before it was too late.

"looking very calm, very dignified"

"out floated Eeyore"

Prioritize on those bothering sorts of days.

ORDER OF LOOKING FOR THINGS

1. Special Place.   (*To find Piglet.*)
2. Piglet.   (*To find who Small is.*)
3. Small.   (*To find Small.*)
4. Rabbit.   (*To tell him I've found Small.*)
5. Small Again.   (*To tell him I've found Rabbit.*)

Christopher Robin came down from the Forest
to the bridge, feeling all sunny and careless,
and just as if twice nineteen didn't matter a bit,
as it didn't on such a happy afternoon, and he thought
that if he stood on the bottom rail of the bridge,
and leant over, and watched the river slipping slowly
away beneath him, then he would suddenly know
everything that there was to be known, and he would
be able to tell Pooh, who wasn't quite sure about some of it.

all sunny and careless

Leave behind the things
that do not matter.

Look on the **bright** side.

"my tail's getting cold"

"I shouldn't be surprised if it hailed
a good deal tomorrow," Eeyore was saying.
"Blizzards and what-not. Being fine today
doesn't Mean Anything."

It might **never** happen!

Piglet's ears . . . streamed behind him . . . like banners

"Supposing a tree fell down, Pooh,
when we were underneath it?"

"Supposing it didn't," said Pooh
after careful thought.

Piglet was comforted by this . . .

CHAPTER THREE

For when you're in a tight place

Find a Thoughtful Spot
of your own.

Halfway between Pooh's house and Piglet's house was a Thoughtful Spot where they met sometimes when they had decided to go and see each other, and as it was warm and out of the wind they would sit down there for a little and wonder what they would do now that they *had* seen each other.

One day when they had decided not to do anything, Pooh made up a verse about it, so that everybody should know what the place was for.

This warm and sunny Spot
Belongs to Pooh.
And here he wonders what
He's going to do.
Oh, bother, I forgot—
It's Piglet's too.

He splashed to his door and looked out. . . . "This is Serious," said Pooh. "I must have an Escape."

So he took his largest pot of honey and escaped with it to a broad branch of his tree, well above the water, and then he climbed down again and escaped with another pot . . . and when the whole Escape was finished, there was Pooh sitting on his branch, dangling his legs, and there, beside him, were ten pots of honey. . . .

Two days later, there was Pooh, sitting on his branch, dangling his legs, and there, beside him, were four pots of honey. . . .

Three days later, there was Pooh, sitting on his branch, dangling his legs, and there, beside him, was one pot of honey.

Four days later, there was Pooh . . .

Time to Escape for a while?

Eleven o'clock will
always cheer you up.

"Took down a very large jar
of honey from the top shelf"

He looked up at his clock, which had stopped
at five minutes to eleven some weeks ago.

"Nearly eleven o'clock," said Pooh happily. "You're
just in time for a little smackerel of something,"
and he put his head into the cupboard. "And then
we'll go out, Piglet, and sing my song to Eeyore."

Recognize when it's time to take a holiday.

"And how are you?" said Winnie-the-Pooh.

Eeyore shook his head from side to side.

"Not very how," he said. "I don't seem to have felt at all how for a long time."

"Dear, dear," said Pooh, "I'm sorry about that. Let's have a look at you."

It helps to air your ideas.

. . . When you are a Bear of Very Little Brain, and you Think of Things, you find sometimes that a Thing which seemed very Thingish inside you is quite different when it gets out into the open and has other people looking at it.

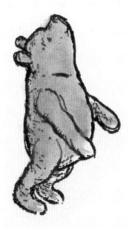

Pooh was so tired when he got home that, in the
very middle of his supper, after he had been eating
for little more than half an hour, he fell fast asleep
in his chair, and slept and slept and slept.

Prevent **complete** exhaustion
with a Pooh **power nap.**

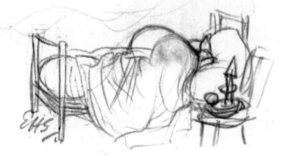

As soon as Rabbit was out of sight, Pooh remembered that he had forgotten to ask who Small was, and whether he was the sort of friend-and-relation who settled on one's nose, or the sort who got trodden on by mistake, and as it was Too Late Now, he thought he would begin the Hunt by looking for Piglet, and asking him what they were looking for before he looked for it.

Make a **note** of
important **details**.

Know when it's time for a new start.

Pooh had wandered into the Hundred Acre Wood,
and was standing in front of what had once been
Owl's House. It didn't look at all like a house now;
it looked like a tree which had been blown down;
and as soon as a house looks like that, it is time
you tried to find another one.

"Come on, Tigger," he called out. "It's easy."

But Tigger was holding on to the branch and saying to himself: "It's all very well for Jumping Animals like Kangas, but it's quite different for Swimming Animals like Tiggers." And he thought of himself floating on his back down a river, or striking out from one island to another, and he felt that that was really the life for a Tigger.

Find the adventure
that suits you.

"What are you doing?"

"I'm planting a haycorn, Pooh, so that it can grow up into an oak-tree, and have lots of haycorns just outside the front door instead of having to walk miles and miles, do you see, Pooh?"

Think long-term.

Indulge in some
do-not-disturb time.

"Is anybody at home?"

There was a sudden scuffling noise from inside the hole, and then silence.

"What I said was, 'Is anybody at home?'" called out Pooh very loudly.

"No!" said a voice; and then added, "You needn't shout so loud. I heard you quite well the first time."

"Bother!" said Pooh. "Isn't there anybody here at all?"

"Nobody."

Can't find what
you're looking for?

Try Pooh's logic...

"How would it be," said Pooh slowly, "if, as soon as we're out of sight of this Pit, we try to find it again?"

"What's the good of that?" said Rabbit.

"Well," said Pooh, "we keep looking for Home and not finding it, so I thought that if we looked for this Pit, we'd be sure not to find it, which would be a Good Thing, because then we might find something that we *weren't* looking for, which might be just what we *were* looking for, really."

Don't dwell on your mistakes.

"I see now," said Winnie-the-Pooh.

"I have been Foolish and Deluded," said he, "and I am a Bear of No Brain at All."

"You're the Best Bear in All the World," said Christopher Robin soothingly.

"Am I?" said Pooh hopefully. And then he brightened up suddenly.

"Anyhow," he said, "it is nearly Luncheon Time."

So he went home for it.

"I shall do it," said Pooh, after waiting a little longer, "by means of a trap. And it must be a Cunning Trap, so you will have to help me, Piglet."

"Pooh," said Piglet, feeling quite happy again now, "I will." And then he said, "How shall we do it?" and Pooh said, "That's just it. How?" And then they sat down together to think it out.

Use your Cunning to
solve problems.

It might **not be** your fault.

"Pooh," said Owl severely, "did *you* do that?"

"'No," said Pooh humbly. "*I* don't *think* so."

"Then who did?"

"*I* think it was the wind," said Piglet. "*I* think your house has blown down."

"Oh, is that it? *I* thought it was Pooh."

"No," said Pooh.

"*If* it was the wind," said Owl, considering the matter, "then it wasn't Pooh's fault. No blame can be attached to him."

Then Pooh had an idea, and I think that
for a Bear of Very Little Brain, it was a
good idea. He said to himself:

"If a bottle can float, then a jar can float,
and if a jar floats, I can sit on the top of it,
if it's a very big jar."

Be **inventive** when
you're in a **tight spot**.

CHAPTER FOUR

For those hummy sort of days

Doing **Nothing**
with your friends
is the **best thing**
in the world.

"What do you like doing best in the world, Pooh?"...

Pooh thought that being with Christopher Robin was a very good thing to do, and having Piglet near was a very friendly thing to have; and so, when he had thought it all out, he said, "What I like best in the whole world is Me and Piglet going to see You, and You saying 'What about a little something?' and Me saying 'Well, I shouldn't mind a little something, should you, Piglet,' and it being a hummy sort of day outside, and birds singing."

"I like that too," said Christopher Robin, "but what I like *doing* best is Nothing."

A friendly paw will reassure.

Piglet sidled up to Pooh from behind.

"Pooh!" he whispered.

"Yes, Piglet?"

"Nothing," said Piglet, taking Pooh's paw. "I just wanted to be sure of you."

Treat yourself

every now and then.

Sing Ho! for the life of a Bear!
Sing Ho! for the life of a Bear!
I don't much mind if it rains or snows,
'Cos I've got a lot of honey on my nice new nose,
I don't much care if it snows or thaws,
'Cos I've got a lot of honey on my nice clean paws!
Sing Ho! for a Bear!
Sing Ho! for a Pooh!
And I'll have a little something in an hour or two!

"It won't break," whispered Pooh comfortingly,
"because you're a Small Animal, and I'll stand underneath,
and if you save us all, it will be a Very Grand Thing to talk
about afterwards, and perhaps I'll make up a Song, and
people will say 'It was so grand what Piglet did that
a Respectful Pooh Song was made about it!'"

Celebrate **others'**
talents too.

Helping someone is a
Grand Thing to do.

So with these words Pooh unhooked it, and carried
it back to Eeyore; and when Christopher Robin
had nailed it on in its right place again, Eeyore
frisked about the forest, waving his tail so happily
that Winnie-the-Pooh came over all funny, and
had to hurry home for a little snack of something
to sustain him. And, wiping his mouth half an
hour afterwards, he sang to himself proudly:

Who found the Tail?
"I," said Pooh,
"At a quarter to two
(Only it was quarter to eleven really),
I found the Tail!"

Keep **an eye** on your **friends' welfare** too.

"I don't know how it is, Christopher Robin, but what with all this snow and one thing and another, not to mention icicles and such-like, it isn't so Hot in my field about three o'clock in the morning as some people think it is. It isn't Close, if you know what I mean—not so as to be uncomfortable. It isn't Stuffy. In fact, Christopher Robin," he went on in a loud whisper, "quite-between-ourselves-and-don't-tell-anybody, it's Cold."

"Oh, Eeyore!"

— It isn't close —   — It isn't stuffy —

"The atmospheric conditions have been very unfavourable lately," said Owl.

"The what?"

"It has been raining," explained Owl.

"Yes," said Christopher Robin. "It has."

"The flood-level has reached an unprecedented height."

"The who?"

"There's a lot of water about," explained Owl.

"Yes," said Christopher Robin, "there is."

"However, the prospects are rapidly becoming more favourable."

Start with **small talk** to
brighten up conversations.

Keep your promises.

"Pooh, *promise* you won't forget
about me, ever. Not even when
I'm a hundred."
  Pooh thought for a little.
  "How old shall I be then?"
  "Ninety-nine."
  Pooh nodded.
  "I promise," he said.

It's wise not to tell secrets.

"Owl," said Christopher Robin, "I am going to give a party."

"You are, are you?" said Owl.

"And it's to be a special sort of party, because it's because of what Pooh did when he did what he did to save Piglet from the flood."

"Oh, that's what it's for, is it?" said Owl.

"Yes, so will you tell Pooh as quickly as you can, and all the others, because it will be tomorrow."

"Oh, it will, will it?" said Owl, still being as helpful as possible.

"So will you go and tell them, Owl?"

Owl tried to think of something very wise to say, but couldn't, so he flew off to tell the others. And the first person he told was Pooh.

Kanga and Roo were spending a quiet afternoon in a
sandy part of the Forest. Baby Roo was practising very
small jumps in the sand, and falling down mouse-holes
and climbing out of them, and Kanga was fidgeting
about and saying "Just one more jump, dear, and then
we must go home." And at that moment who should
come stumping up the hill but Pooh.

"Good afternoon, Kanga."

"Good afternoon, Pooh."

"Look at me jumping," squeaked Roo,
and fell into another mouse-hole.

Some of the **best fun**

in life is free.

Christopher Robin sat at one end, and Pooh sat at the other, and between them on one side were Owl and Eeyore and Piglet,

Take **more** meals together.

and between them
on the other side were Rabbit, and
Roo and Kanga. And all Rabbit's friends-
and-relations spread themselves about on the
grass, and waited hopefully in case anybody
spoke to them, or dropped anything, or asked
them the time.

"Oh, Bear!" said Christopher Robin.

"How I do love you!"

"So do I," said Pooh.

You are **very lovable**—
love yourself!

"Pooh!" squeaked the voice.

"It's Piglet!" cried Pooh eagerly.
"Where are you?"

"Underneath," said Piglet in an underneath sort of way.

"Underneath what?"

"You," squeaked Piglet. "Get up!"

"Oh!" said Pooh, and scrambled up as quickly as
he could. "Did I fall on you, Piglet?"

"You fell on me," said Piglet, feeling himself all over.

"I didn't mean to," said Pooh sorrowfully.

"I didn't mean to be underneath," said Piglet sadly.
"But I'm all right now, Pooh, and I am so glad it was you."

Good friends are always pleased to see you.

Pooh and his friends will **always be there** for you.

But, of course, it isn't really Good-bye, because the Forest will always be there . . . and anybody who is Friendly with Bears can find it.

In that enchanted place on the top of the Forest, a little boy and his Bear will always be playing.